# MEOW MONDAY

Phyllis Root

illustrated by
Helen Craig

CANDLEWICK PRESS
CAMBRIDGE, MASSACHUSETTS

One Monday,
Bonnie Bumble's pussy willows
all burst into bloom.

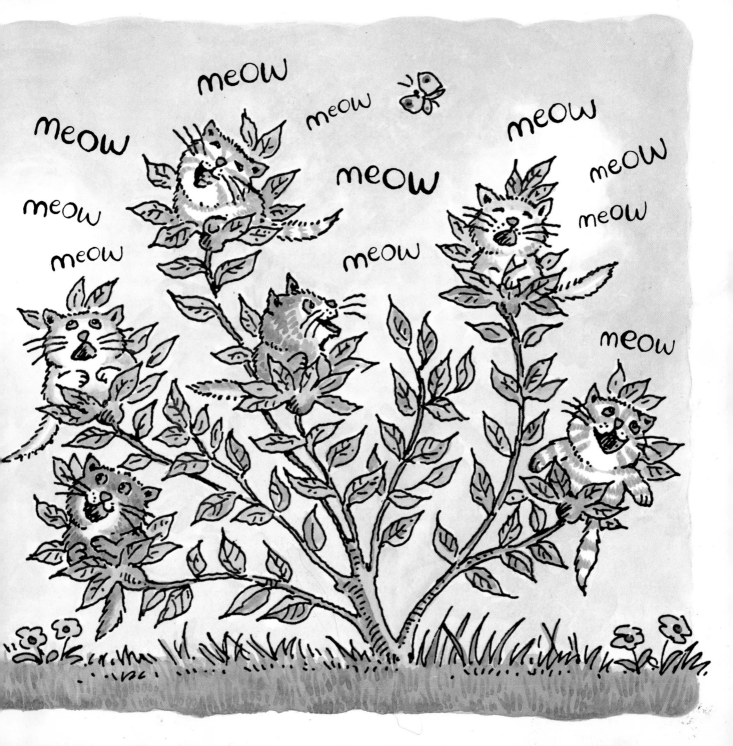

They raised such a ruckus
the hen stopped laying.

The cow wouldn't give milk.

And the pig and the sheep
covered their ears.

"This ruckus can't go on!"
said Bonnie Bumble.

meOW meOW meow
meOW
meOW

She fed the pussy willows
cat food and catnip.

meow
meow
meow
meow
meow
meow

She petted them
and brushed them.

She gave them a ball of yarn.
But nothing worked.

At last Bonnie remembered
the milkweed growing
beside the barn.

It was just what the pussy willows wanted.

purrrr

Purr

purr

Purr

Purrrrr

Purr

purrr

Pu

Pur

Purrrrr

Purr

purrr

Purrr

r

Purrrr

purr

purrrr

Purr

When they were full,
the pussy willows all
curled up for a catnap.

It was so peaceful
the hen laid an egg.

The cow gave milk.

And the pig
and the sheep
uncovered their ears.

"Quiet at last,"
sighed Bonnie Bumble.

And it was . . .

until the dogwood started to bloom.

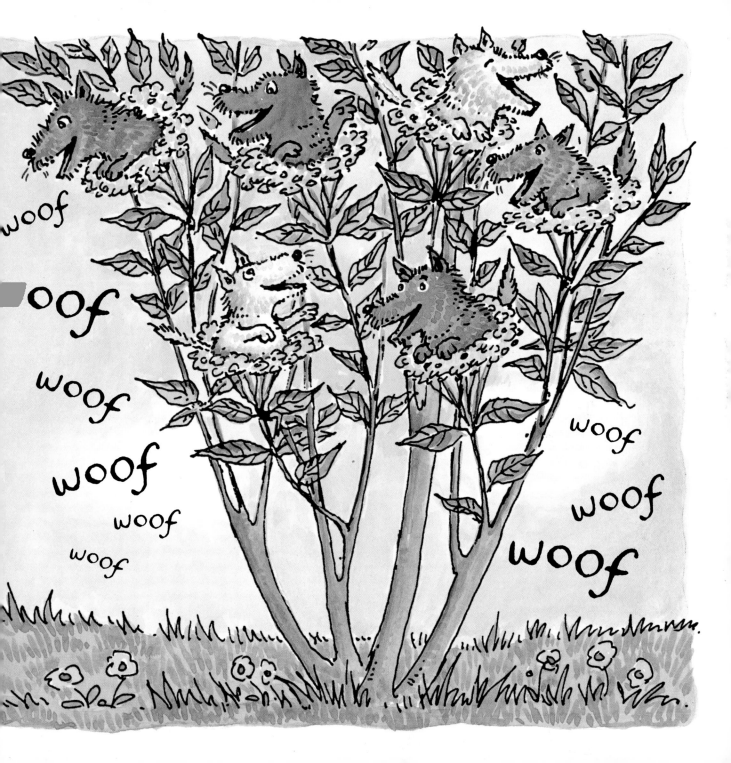

Text copyright © 2000 by Phyllis Root
Illustrations copyright © 2000 by Helen Craig

First edition 2000

Library of Congress Cataloging-in-Publication Data

Root, Phyllis, date.
Meow Monday / Phyllis Root ; illustrated by Helen Craig
—1st ed.
p.  cm.
Summary: When her pussy willows burst into bloom and
raise a ruckus which upsets the farm animals, Bonnie tries
to find a way to quiet the meowing shrub.
ISBN 0-7636-0832-7 (hardcover)
ISBN 0-7636-0831-9 (paperback)
[1. Pussy willow—Fiction. 2. Farm life—Fiction.]
I. Craig, Helen, ill. II. Title.
PZ7. R6784Me    2001
[E]—dc21    99-047078

10 9 8 7 6 5 4 3 2 1

Printed in Hong Kong

Candlewick Press
2067 Massachusetts Avenue
Cambridge, Massachusetts 02140

woof

wo